DATE DUE

Demco, Inc. 38-293

TUK AND THE WHALE

TUK and the WHALE

*

Raquel Rivera

PICTURES BY
Mary Jane Gerber

GROUNDWOOD BOOKS / HOUSE OF ANANSI PRESS
TORONTO BERKELEY

Groundwood Books / House of Anansi Press
110 Spadina Avenue, Suite 801, Toronto, Ontario M5V 2K4
or c/o Publishers Group West
1700 Fourth Street, Berkeley, CA 94710

We acknowledge for their financial support of our publishing
program the Canada Council for the Arts, the Government of Canada
through the Book Publishing Industry Development Program (BPIDP)
and the Ontario Arts Council.

Library and Archives Canada Cataloguing in Publication
Rivera, Raquel
Tuk and the whale / authored by Raquel Rivera ; illustrated by Mary
Jane Gerber.
ISBN-13: 978-0-88899-689-3 (bound).–
ISBN-10: 0-88899-689-6 (bound).
ISBN-13: 978-0-88899-891-0 (pbk.)–
ISBN-10: 0-88899-891-0 (pbk.)
I. Gerber, Mary Jane II. Title.
PS8635.I9435T83 2008   jC813'.6   C2007-907124-4

Design by Michael Solomon
Printed in Canada

For Kim Sang

1

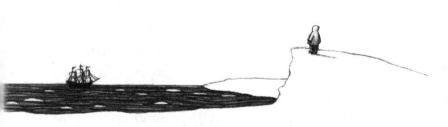

Grandfather suddenly stopped working.

He had been drilling holes through a flat piece of driftwood. Wood was a rare find. This piece would fill another gap between the sled runners of the family's kamotiq.

Now he sat perfectly still. His bow-drill stopped spinning.

Tuk watched while Grandfather slowly leaned back on his heels. Did the old man hear something? Tuk strained his ears. All he could hear was the *whump-whump* of a raven's wings beating at the wind.

"They are here," said Grandfather. He went back to work, spinning the drill shaft deeper into the wood.

Tuk's eyes widened.

They are here! Just the way Grandfather had dreamed. Tuk had to see this. He jumped up and ran toward the beach, stumbling over the snow-covered rocks.

"Sure, go," Grandfather said to the air. "He's young. He gets excited."

Tuk climbed the crest that protected their camp from the wind. He reached the top and looked out over the bay.

There was the beach, cleared of snow by strong winds off the water. The sea ice stretched into the bay. It broke up into floes at the far edge.

Nothing unusual to see here. He waited a moment. Grandfather was hardly ever wrong.

There it was!

It looked like two great narwhal horns rising from the water, piercing straight through the sky. Tuk squinted against the glare that bounced off the ice. Those flapping white skins must be the "sails" Grandfather had mentioned. He said they could be turned to catch the wind, or turned away when the wind was too fierce.

Next into view came the great hull. It was the biggest boat Tuk had ever seen. What kind of creatures would travel in such a large boat? They must be giants!

Tuk felt a chill.

"Mother!" he called, even though he knew she couldn't hear him. He turned and ran all the way back to camp.

Mother was outside the snowhouse. She was chewing on a scraped sealskin, making it soft enough to sew.

"Mother, when is Father coming back?" Tuk gasped as he reached her side.

"The light is still strong," she replied. "He may return today."

"Because the boat is coming! The boat that Grandfather dreamed about! I can see it already. Tomorrow it will be here!"

Mother put down the skin, but her mouth stayed open. She stood up, looking this way and that.

"Unat," Mother called out for Tuk's sister. "Where are you? You know I don't like you to run off alone!"

"I'm just here, Mother!" Tuk's little sister was on the other side of the iglu's entry porch, playing with a rock. She had tied a rabbit skin around it to make a baby doll.

Mother turned back to Tuk. "And you, did you leave your grandfather by himself, when he needs your help?"

"Don't worry, Mother, the boat won't be here for a while. It is still far away."

"No, it is not far away," Mother said half to herself. She looked toward the coast. "I wish your father would return," she murmured.

"I'm going to find Samik. He'll want to see this!" Tuk told her.

"I want to come!" Unat called, looking up from her doll.

Tuk turned to Mother, who said, "Keep

her with you. Make sure she comes back. I want her staying with us tonight."

Unat had a good friend in every iglu, and she often slept away from home. Even Maakut, who was a camp elder, sometimes invited Unat to stay. But Unat's favorite place was her best friend Ooleepeeka's iglu.

Ooleepeeka had two mothers. Her father was such a good hunter that he needed two wives to take care of the skins. So Ooleepeeka lived with more brothers and sisters than anyone Tuk and Unat knew. When it was too dark and cold to play outside, there were always games and songs in Ooleepeeka's iglu.

Tuk's best friend in camp was Samik.

Samik was the youngest in his family, about the same age as Tuk. His mother and father were quite old now. His brothers and sisters had husbands, wives and children of their own.

"Come on, Unat, I know where we can find him," Tuk said. Samik would be some-where along the river with his throwing bones. Sometimes he brought back a ptarmigan or a rabbit.

Unat was out of breath. It was hard to keep up with her brother's big steps in the snow.

"Tuk, why does the boat come to bother us?"

"Don't be scared of the boat," Tuk said. "Remember Grandfather's dream? He said a great skinless boat will appear from over the sea. And it will leak out treasures from the land of things."

"Yes, but what does that mean?"

"I don't know," Tuk admitted. "But Grandfather would tell us if there was anything to be scared about, right?"

"I guess," Unat said. But she didn't sound so sure.

Tuk didn't say it, but he wasn't so sure, either.

The children's thoughts were soon interrupted by distant shouts of laughter. They looked at each other. Samik wasn't hunting, not with all that shouting. He must have gone sliding!

Unat let out a whoop and ran toward the noise. Tuk followed.

Samik and Ooleepeeka were flying down over the snow humps and boulders of Steep Hill. They rode on the skin of a bearded seal. It made sliding so much faster. They tumbled off it as they reached the bottom.

"I want to go next!" Unat shouted as soon as she reached them. But Ooleepeeka's big sister Arna was waiting her turn.

"Unat, you're too little to slide Steep Hill," Arna said.

"I am not! I'm almost as big as Ooleepeeka!"

"Forget the hill," Tuk said. "The boat, the great boat is coming into the bay! Grandfather said it would, and now it has come!"

The group ran over crusty snow and rocky ground. They crept up the crest. They peered over the ridge.

"Ooooee," breathed Samik. "How many people must fit in that boat?"

"Grandfather dreamed that it is not a boat

full of people. He thinks it is mostly empty," said Tuk. "He says they want to fill it."

"Fill it with what?" Ooleepeeka asked. Tuk shrugged.

"My father says we should stop the boat when it comes," Samik said. "It should go somewhere that is empty, like we did. Father says we should fight and drive it away. After all," he added, "that boat brings strangers."

Samik was right. Strangers couldn't be trusted. They weren't related by blood, or by marriage. They didn't bring news of friends and family in other camps. They could take things, break things — even hurt people. It was easy for strangers to do bad things to people because they didn't know anyone. And they could always just leave again.

Tuk and the others stayed under the shelter of the ridge after that. They threw stones to see who could throw the farthest. Every so often someone would climb up to make sure that the boat was still far out in the bay.

The days were so long now. It was almost never dark. Nobody slept much during this time. The sun kept them all awake.

Finally, the daylight dipped behind the hills. When it was too dark to see the frosty breath in front of their faces, everyone began to get cold and tired.

Maybe their fathers had come back from hunting. Maybe they had caught seals.

"Let's go," Tuk nudged Unat, whose face kept dropping into the fluffy trim on her parka. "You are falling asleep on your feet."

Everyone started back, guided home by the camp snowhouses. Each iglu glowed like a moon in the blue night. The qulliit were lit. Even if there was no meat, they would soon be snug and warm.

As Tuk and his sister neared their home, he saw humps in the snow drifts.

"The dogs!" Tuk whispered.

"Father's back!" Unat cried.

"Shhh!" Tuk hushed her, pointing toward the bright iglu. He could hear several voices.

They had visitors. Surely the grown-ups

had gathered to decide what should be done about the strange boat in the bay.

In the dark outside, Tuk spoke softly into Unat's ear.

"Stay quiet as we go in. Head straight for the sleeping platform. Don't say anything."

Children weren't really supposed to listen to conversations between their elders. But Tuk was almost grown now. He didn't want Unat's baby ways to get them both sent away.

The two of them skirted around the dogs. Father had tied them separately to keep them from fighting. One or two looked up, but they didn't bark. They knew the two children creeping past.

Tuk eased Unat's small form into the main room, guiding her quietly toward the back. He knew that the grown-ups were aware of their entrance. He just hoped that they couldn't be bothered to interrupt themselves and send them to another iglu.

"Your dream says they are not evil spirits," said a low voice, Samik's father. "They are ordinary men — just Qallunaat. We can drive them away. We have done this before. The stories say so."

Samik's father crossed his arms, tucking his hands up into his sleeves. "What about the time those strangers raided the camp at Bloody Point? What about that story? And don't forget the story about the curious hunter who paddled too close. The Qallunaat pulled him right out of the water into their great boat, his kayak still attached! No one ever saw the hunter again. We should get them — before they get us."

"There are other stories," Maakut's son said. "Stories of peaceful trading and friend-ship." Long ago, Maakut had adopted her nephew's baby. Now that he was a young hunter, Maakut's son could feed his adop-tive mother, as she had fed and cared for him.

"That is right," Grandfather replied. "We know those stories, too. The dream said that we should help the strangers from the great boat."

"But why, Arvik?" asked Maakut. "Are they too many to fight?"

Of all the grown-ups in camp, Maakut was the only one older than Grandfather. It was right that she be the one to question him.

"They are many," Grandfather admitted. "And they have no women or children to feed and protect. It is better for our families if we don't fight. The dream said that they would ask for help and, if we help them, they will go away again."

"We are busy. And we need our food for ourselves," Ooleepeeka's father pointed out.

"That is true. But they bring their own provisions from far away. In that respect, they can take care of themselves." Grandfather had an answer for everyone.

"If we share our meat, maybe they will share, too," Maakut mused.

Samik's father was still. They would do as Grandfather said.

2

THE next morning, Tuk buried himself deep under the sleeping furs when Mother tried to wake him up.

"Tuk, come and check the traps with us," she urged, shaking his foot. It was the only part she could find among the mound of furs. "Unat and I could use the help."

Tuk pulled his foot back into hiding. Mother didn't need his help. She was just worried about leaving him behind. The boat was landing today. Father and Grandfather had already left the iglu, and Tuk was sure they were going to meet the strangers.

But Tuk was too big to be bossed by his mother. He had other plans for today.

"Okay, lazy-head, you sleep. Unat and I will eat meat without you."

And with that, Tuk heard them leave.

Quickly he kicked away the covers and struggled into his trousers, the ones with the fur on the inside. He spent precious moments looking for his boots before he found them behind the qulliq. He slid his feet into the soft kamiit that kept them warm and dry. He hopped into his sealskin outer trousers and his parka that were hanging by the porch doorway.

Now he was ready to catch up with the men.

He could see them at the ice edge. The great boat was anchored out in the bay. But several strangers had used a small boat to row in. There were a few more of these small boats strapped to the sides of the bigger boat.

The small boats reminded Tuk of the umiak his family traveled in during summer time, when the ice was gone. Umiat were sometimes called women's boats because the women rowed them with oars, while the hunters paddled alongside in their kayaks.

But the strangers' boat was different. There were no sealskins stretched over its frame. It was made entirely of wood. With the umiak, they had to be sure not to scrape holes in the skin covering. But a boat like this one, all wood — this boat must be very strong. The Qallunaat were lucky to find so much wood.

Tuk could see that Father, Grandfather and the other men of the camp were standing back from the strangers. One of the strangers was talking and waving his arms. The rest of them huddled together. The hunters held themselves tight, ready for any sudden moves.

It was too late to back out now. Tuk ran out to join the group on the sea ice.

As he approached, Tuk watched the

strangers. They had so much hair on their faces, like bears! And their clothes were so flimsy. The wind flattened their coats right against their bodies. Why didn't they wear furs? Perhaps their bodies were already covered in fur, the same as their faces.

Tuk stopped in his tracks.

Father turned to him and frowned. Grandfather signaled for Tuk to stand next to him. Tuk was glad for that. Up close, these Qallunaat were very tall. They were pale, too. Even their hair was pale. And they smelled terrible. Grandfather said that creatures smelled of what they ate. Did these strangers eat rotten eggs? Did they drink dog urine?

At the sight of Tuk, the strangers' attitude changed. The one who was talking smiled and spoke to him. Tuk had no idea what the Qallunaaq was saying. He stepped behind his grandfather. The stranger laughed, but not in a mean way.

Father tried out some different words. He had traveled far and could speak the words of many different people. He tried words from the people of the cold islands. Then he tried words used by people of the coast far beyond.

Then the talking stranger spoke a few words. He said two that father had heard before, from people who had blown from over the sea.

"Pot," the stranger said. "Fire."

"Good words," Father said.

"Arvik," the stranger said. "Whale."

Father turned to Grandfather, eyebrows raised. Arvik was Tuk's grandfather's name. Arvik was also the great black whale. No animal was bigger or more powerful than Arvik.

The Qallunaat were waving and pointing at the water.

"What are they talking about?" Samik's father asked.

"Maybe they saw a whale," Ooleepeeka's father suggested.

"Maybe they're hungry," said Maakut's son. "Maybe they like to eat whale, too."

Tuk had never eaten the great black whale. Arvik was risky to hunt, a monster of an animal, the biggest of them all. It was difficult to manage a hunt like that. Tuk's mother preferred that Father hunt smaller animals, like beluga and narwhal. She even pretended she preferred the taste of their maktaaq, even though everyone else agreed that the skin of the great black whale was the most delicious of all.

THUMP!

Tuk was startled out of his thoughts by a great big Qallunaaq hand reaching out and landing — *smack* — on the top of his head, tousling his hair all over.

Tuk made a face and all the men smiled, even Father. Again, the Qallunaaq was talking to him. This time Tuk raised his eyebrows and looked at Father. The stranger laughed and pushed something into Tuk's hand.

It had a wooden handle. It wasn't driftwood, either. It was harder and more shiny. But the best part was the other end. It was sharp. And it wasn't made from bone, tusk or stone flint. It looked like it was made from iron metal — like Father's special spear tips.

Could it be? Tuk knelt down over his kamik and pulled out a long thick lace made from the toughest bearded seal hide. He cut right through it, almost as if the lace had always been two.

It was a knife!

And what a knife! He looked up at the men circled around him, hunters and Qallunaat. This time everyone broke out laughing at the expression on his face. Father asked to look at the knife. Tuk's gift was passed among the hunters and returned safely back to his hands.

Talk erupted on both sides. Things were friendly now. Tuk turned the knife over and over. What a strong tool it was — strong like their small boat. These Qallunaat might look and smell odd, but they made wonderful things.

But wait, what was happening? Tuk had been so absorbed with his gift, he didn't notice that Father was going off in the little boat with the strangers.

"Father!" he cried.

"He wants to see the great boat," Grandfather said. He put his hand on Tuk's shoulder. "Everything will be fine. Look, Ooleepeeka's father is going with him. They want to see what else the Qallunaat have to trade." Tuk saw that two of the Qallunaat were staying behind. He supposed they would be taken back to the big boat when Father returned.

"Everything will be fine," Grandfather said for the second time. But his brow was furrowed.

Tuk's heart raced as he watched his father being rowed out to the big boat. It wasn't like Father to go off without his own kayak. Was it Tuk's knife that had caused him to do this? The knife lay so comfortably in his hand. It was hard not to love it. Tuk stared at its sharp edge and willed his father to come back.

"Your father is coming back." Grandfather spoke aloud Tuk's silent thoughts. Then Grandfather exchanged glances with the other two hunters. Should they take the two

strangers back to camp — to the wives and the children?

There was a pause. Somebody coughed. Nobody knew what to do next. Grandfather shrugged.

"Let's invite our visitors back to camp, then."

As their group approached the camp, Tuk had a chance to examine the two strangers more closely. They smelled frightened. But how could that be? They must be very powerful and wise to guide the great boat anchored in the bay. They must be strong, too. They didn't even wear furs in the cold. Tuk wondered about the long stick each one carried so close to his side. Maybe they were spears. But they didn't look sharp.

The whole camp gathered around to see the strangers that the hunters had brought back from the sea. The Qallunaat gave out beads of marvelous colors: fire, moss, bright sky on a beautiful day. What pretty gifts!

"You are so lucky!" Samik cried when Tuk

showed him the knife. "You should have told me you were sneaking off to meet the strangers!"

"I would have forbidden you to join him." Samik's father was behind them. "The strangers make good weapons," he said, eyeing Tuk's knife. "They are not our friends. It is easy to smile and give small gifts."

But watching the Qallunaat now, it was hard to imagine that they meant any harm. One of them was chasing Unat and Ooleepeeka all around the camp, pretending to try to catch them. The girls squealed and screamed, but he always tripped and fell down at the last minute. Even the grown-ups laughed and clapped. They all seemed to agree that maybe these strangers were not so bad after all.

Grandfather made a sign to bring the visitors to his family's iglu.

"No, Father!" Mother called out from the front porch of the snowhouse. "Don't bring those creatures in here! Wait, I am coming out." Mother emerged outside, her face a knot of worry. The friendly Qallunaaq, now red-faced and puffing hard, offered her some beads.

Mother was impressed. She had never seen anything like these. She held them up to the sun and saw how they caught the light. These could be sewn on to Unat's hood. It would be beautiful.

"Daughter, invite the visitors inside your house, won't you? They are waiting for your husband to return from the boat."

Mother hesitated, and then gestured her welcome.

The Qallunaat's faces clouded over. They didn't seem very happy. They tightened their grip on their spears.

At this moment, the family's lead dog leapt up from his place, snarling and barking. The Qallunaat jumped back, spears ready. But Grandfather spoke to the dog, starting with a low growl from the back of his throat.

"Keeeeelut, get down! Or I'll bite off your nose!" Keelut was a strong puller, and smart, like a lead dog should be. But sometimes he had to be reminded who was the boss.

Keelut backed away, turned a few times and lay down. The Qallunaat crouched down and followed Mother into the front porch, one after the other. Grandfather came close behind. All the children who could possibly squeeze into the iglu followed, too.

A stone pot of ptarmigan stew bubbled over the qulliq.

"Unat and I were extra lucky this morning. Our traps caught many birds."

Mother placed a large dish on the clean snow floor. Steam rose from the rich broth. Someone's belly gave a loud growl. It was one of the strangers. His eyes were big over the bowl. Grandfather reached in and chose a dripping piece of meat. Delicious! He gestured that the strangers should do the same. Mother handed the antler spoon to Tuk.

"Not that you deserve any, lazy-head!" But she was smiling as she said it.

Tuk scooped up some of the gravy dotted with fat and the odd white feather. He took a long drink from it, and passed the spoon on.

The first stranger gulped down two big spoonfuls of soup before the second took it from him. They wolfed down their meat. Food and gravy became stuck in their beards. The children watched them, wide-eyed.

"These strangers are not well." Mother whispered to Tuk. "Look at how that one's bones show. And how the other has skin that sags, as if he was much fatter not long ago. They have been sick. They haven't been eating proper food."

Tuk shrugged while he gnawed the meat off a neck bone. Maybe that's why Qallunaat looked and smelled the way they did.

When they had finished their meal, Mother cleared the dish away. She scraped out the gravy spots on the floor and put down some clean snow.

The friendly Qallunaaq opened the sack he wore tied around his middle. He pulled out a number of miracles. He showed them two pots, one with a special pouring spout.

The other visitor used it to pretend he was melting snow and then pouring out the water. A kettle-pot, he called it. Both the pot and the kettle-pot were made of a shiny metal the color of the sun.

Tuk was allowed to hold the kettle-pot. It was much lighter than stone. And it would never break. Mother's face was as still as a mask, but Tuk knew she had to be excited by these things.

Then the stranger held up a small sliver. It looked like a needle, only shiny. It must be more metal. The friendly Qallunaaq threaded one with the finest, most flexible sinew Tuk had ever seen. The stranger offered it to Mother.

Mother ran the floppy sinew through two thicknesses of her parka. She couldn't help smiling. Even Tuk could see how smoothly the metal slid through, compared to Mother's bone needle.

The friendly stranger held up two needles along with the kettle. He pointed to the polar bear skin that covered the sleeping platform.

He wanted to trade. Tuk's mother shook her head. Who knew when Father would meet with another polar bear? They needed that skin to protect them from the hard-packed snow of their sleeping platform.

Poor Mother. Tuk knew it cost her a great deal to say no to those needles.

The trader looked around and spied a pile of rabbit skins — mostly old baby shirts from when Unat was little. He pointed at them.

"Help yourself." Mother gestured that he could take them. She turned to Tuk.

"Maybe because they have white skin, they value white furs," she said.

3

S NUG inside the iglu that night, the whole family was together again. Mother told Father about her encounter with the Qallunaat.

"I think they wanted me to sew for them," she told him. "Is it true that they have no wives on their boat?"

"No wives," he replied. "And they have lost some men. I think they have had some trouble on the water. They want our help."

"They look sick," said Mother. "They need good food."

"Here, taste this." Unat handed her mother something that looked like a chalky stone. "They gave me some of their food. It's different. It's crunchy."

"It tastes strange," Mother smacked her lips. "It crumbles like dry earth. You can't live on this. You need meat."

"Maybe that's why they need us," Grandfather guessed. "They want to catch Arvik. Your husband and the others agreed to help them."

Tuk turned to Father. Could it be true? Father hadn't hunted the great black whale since Tuk could remember. If Father was going to help catch Arvik, there would be enough food for everyone! And Tuk would taste the delicious maktaaq for the first time.

"They hunt Arvik across the sea," Father explained. "Storms and ice pushed them this way. They plan to return to their own land, but they want to take back any whales they can find in these waters."

It was true! Father was going to hunt Arvik, just like in the stories!

"I want to help!" Tuk blurted out, almost before he even had the thought.

"Sure, you'll go." Father told him. Mother sucked in her breath.

"Me, too!" Unat cried.

"Don't be a foolish little girl!" Mother sounded angry.

"Tuk is almost a young man now," Grandfather said. "He needs to learn things if he's going to be a hunter like his father."

Father was quiet. He picked up a small stone.

"I think I see a small puppy in here," he said.

Unat's trembling lip turned up into a little smile.

"I will make you a puppy for your baby doll," Father declared.

He began to carve.

"That's a good knife you got this morning, Tuk," Father said. "It's a tool for a hunter, not a boy. You understand?"

"I think so, Father." Tuk felt serious, though he wasn't sure why. He also wasn't really sure what Father wanted him to understand. But he wasn't going to ask. Father might think he wasn't ready to go on the hunt.

"Grandfather, tell us a story about the whale hunt," Unat asked.

"Humph," Father cleared his throat. "Dogs need to be fed," he muttered as he made his way out into the night.

Grandfather waited until Father was outside.

"He's worried," he told the others. "He prefers to hunt from a kayak, not this umiak boat the Qallunaat use. But the Qallunaat want us to go with them in their boat. I think it will be all right. Our ancestors preferred to hunt whale with umiat and they were very good whale hunters. Our ancestors lived in great houses made of whalebone and stone. They didn't travel all winter and summer the way we do now. But that was before, when the water was warmer and there were more whales."

"Tell us about when Father hunted whale," Tuk urged.

"Yes!" Unat bounced up and down. "Tell us about the time he caught the great black whale!"

Grandfather pulled Unat to him and tickled her red cheeks.

"Well, little one, your father has caught a whale or two, and he has lost a whale or two. But he didn't do it alone. It takes many hunters to bring down Arvik. I heard of only one man who brought in Arvik all by himself. He was your friend Ooleepeeka's great-grandfather."

Grandfather gazed into the lamp fire for a time. Then he spoke, as if to the flame.

"One fine spring morning, Ooleepeeka's great-grandfather crawled out of his tiny iglu on the sea ice. He was planning to hunt seals. But out on the open water he saw many whales. This was a surprise. It had been a long time since Arvik had swum through those waters. Wouldn't it be a wonderful treat for everyone back at camp if he could bring one in!"

That lone hunter must have been very brave. Tuk hoped that he might also be brave on the whale hunt tomorrow.

"The hunter had brought his harpoon and yearling floats to catch a seal. But he could use these same tools to hunt a great whale instead. One float will keep a harpooned seal from sinking deep into the sea. Many floats tied to a line would do the same with Arvik. The hunter had extra lead for his dogs. He tied his floats along this lead. Now he was ready.

"Ooleepeeka's great-grandfather launched his kayak off the edge of the ice. He carried his harpoon, his spear and the line with the yearling floats attached. He paddled his kayak out to the whales."

Grandfather paused. Unat had fallen asleep. He grunted as he shifted her into a more comfortable position. Mother poured him some bone soup. Tuk noticed that Father had slipped back inside.

"And then what happened?" Tuk said.

"When he reached the whales, the hunter

stopped paddling. He let himself drift quietly among them. He chose his whale, one near the edge of the group. He guided his kayak nearer. He waited. He waited a long time so the whale would get used to him. The hunter needed to position himself in the right spot before he struck. He would try to hit just behind the front flipper."

"Because a hurt flipper will make swimming harder," Tuk said.

Grandfather nodded. "And that would help the hunter. He needed all the help he could get. Even if the hunter did everything just right, the whale might get away. But if he was patient, if he was strong, if he was skilled and, most important —" Grandfather raised one finger in the air, "— if he was lucky, he just might bring back a whale for everyone."

Tuk, Mother and Father all smiled.

"Now, the hunter knew he had to gain the trust of the whale, so he sang a nice song."

Grandfather chanted:

"Beautiful whale, you are shiny and fat
Oh, beautiful whale, I will take you back
Beautiful whale, please feed my family and
*   me*
Beautiful whale, we will eat for a whole
*   year."*

"When the hunter was quite sure that the time was right — that the whale was ready — he swiftly paddled his kayak right up on top of the great black body and drove his harpoon deep into Arvik.

"The hunter had to paddle backward — very fast — as the whale shook and rocked in shock and pain. He watched for the tail. Arvik's body moves quite slowly. But the massive tail can flip out of the water in a blink. At any moment he might be crushed by a blow from that tail. Or he might be swatted up to the sky, still attached to his kayak. Or the tail might lash and toss the waves, drenching the hunter in freezing seawater.

"Yes, the hunter watched the tail closely,

paddling this way and that. He searched the glittering surface of the water for signs of the whale's next move."

Grandfather sighed.

Sometimes it made Grandfather sad to tell stories. He said it made him think of the people who had taught him the stories, and how they were no longer here to tell them instead.

He took a breath and continued.

"Then Arvik dived to escape. But the hunter's yearling floats were full of air. They pulled against the whale, toward the surface, where the hunter could see them. Meanwhile, the barbs on the harpoon head stuck fast in the whale's flesh. With every move Arvik made, the needle-sharp point drove the harpoon deeper and deeper.

"And so began a long game between the two — Arvik leading, the hunter following. The hunter mustn't get too close. He must keep out of range of that great tail. But he must not lose track of the whale, either. Sometimes they would go so fast, the hunter's paddle sprayed salt water into his eyes. Sometimes Arvik rested, and they would go slowly. At these times the hunter would sing to the whale:

"There, there, Arvik
Be still, Arvik
My harpoon is in you now
Don't fight, Arvik
Time is right, Arvik
To give yourself over now."

"You see," Grandfather explained, "the hunter was trying to calm the whale, so that he would surface again. A whale can go a very long time under water with just one breath. But eventually he has to come up again. The hunter sensed his chance approaching. He paddled wide around the reach of the tail. He was in position. The whale broke the surface. The whale's breath shot steam into the cold air. As Arvik sucked in another breath, the hunter struck low on the body.

....

"Quick with the killing spear, stab and stab again! Strike at Arvik's lungs, his giant's heart! Speed the injuries and put a quicker end to this great animal!"

The light had grown low in the iglu. The air was cold. Mother broke up a lump of seal fat on the qulliq, using her little pounder to arrange it for the fire. The flames rose higher, casting shadows around Grandfather's eyes.

"It takes time to kill a creature that big, that strong. The hunter was out on the water for a long while. He had to wait for Arvik to tire and die. When he could, he would add to Arvik's injuries. When he could not, he would follow and wait."

That hunter must have been very strong, Tuk thought. He wished he might be strong like that for tomorrow's whale hunt.

"Finally, Arvik's blowhole spouted blood instead of water, and he stopped fighting. His still body tossed among the waves. The hunter followed the whale to shore on the incoming tide."

Everyone in the iglu was quiet. The whale had been caught a long time ago. It was just a story now.

But Tuk was sure everyone was thinking the same thing. Wasn't it a miracle that the whale had finally given itself up to the hunter? And what a wonderful relief that the hunter would live and hunt for his family again.

"And then there was a feast!" Tuk exclaimed.

"And then there was a feast." Grandfather smiled. "But first the whale had to be taken apart. This took many families many days. The hunters cut large notches into Arvik's sides, one above the other, so they could climb up to the top. They cut off great sheets of glistening skin, black on the outside, white on the inside.

"What a taste! Rich, fresh and salty from the sea! Everyone feasted. Whale meat was given to the dogs. The leftovers were stored under great piles of rocks for times of hunger. The bones made tent supports, sled runners, tools and dishes. The story traveled far and the people came from all over to help share the whale and taste the most delicious of all maktaaq. The story was told over and over again by our parents to us. And then it was told by us to our children… and our grandchildren, if they should ever listen." Grandfather gave Unat's snoring head a friendly nudge.

"Yes, Unat," Grandfather addressed the sleeping child. "Your friend Ooleepeeka's great-grandfather was a very lucky man."

4

"A REN'T you coming?" Tuk asked Samik. Almost everybody was heading to shore to see the men and the strangers off on their hunt. But Samik was staying behind.

"No, I have to help Father pack the sled." Samik replied.

"Why? Where are you going?" This was disappointing news. Tuk wanted Samik to hunt with him. After all, Tuk was big enough to learn. Samik could learn, too.

"Don't look at me like that," Samik said. "Father says he won't put my life at risk for strangers. He thinks the hunt will fail. And he's expecting trouble from the Qallunaat. We are going to fetch my brothers and sisters and their families. He says we may need more people to defend ourselves."

"When you return, you'll see there was no need for that. Then you will have missed the hunt for nothing!" Tuk exclaimed. He ran off to catch up with the others.

But as he reached the hunters, a thought crept into his head.

What if Samik's father was right?

Father nodded when Tuk told him what Samik had said.

"Samik's father is cautious," he said. "But if our hunting goes well, I think he will change his mind."

Everyone reached the floe edge.

"It is good to have more people with us, whatever happens," Ooleepeeka's father said. "The strangers want more hunters. They want to catch as many whales as they can."

"I think one whale is enough for us all," Maakut's son said.

"They have a big room inside their boat," Ooleepeeka's father explained. "They want to fill it with whale fat. They must have a lot of qulliit where they come from."

In the distance, Tuk could see the Qallunaat lower one of their small boats off the side of the big one.

Father spoke. "They said they lost many hunters in umiat, out on the water. Two boats full of hunters, they said." He turned to Ooleepeeka's father. "If it is true, that is a great loss."

Tuk realized that all of the Qallunaat small boats might soon be filled with friends and relatives, helping the strangers hunt.

Suddenly, it seemed as if they were going to a great deal of trouble to help these strangers. They couldn't possibly eat all that skin and meat. Why were they risking their lives?

"If we catch enough whales, they will give us one of their boats," Father said, as if he could hear Tuk's thoughts.

....

"They have other beautiful things, too," Ooleepeeka's father added. "We must trade for them. Axes, pounders and spears of all kinds — made with metal, very strong."

Tuk's hand went to his new knife. He kept it safe in the pocket he hung around his neck, inside his parka.

Ooleepeeka's father said, "Still, it would be better if we had more hunters. Many boats against Arvik would be better. "They have many men on that great boat, even if they lost some. They could fill more umiat."

"I think those others just stay on the great boat. I don't think they know how to hunt," Father replied.

Tuk and Maakut's son looked at each other, eyes wide. Not know how to hunt! But if a man doesn't know how to hunt, he can't get married, have a family! Such a man is a most unfortunate soul. Could this be why they had no women on their great boat?

"Anyway, one boat can catch Arvik. There are three of us," Father offered. "And Tuk is helping, and those two Qallunaat coming now."

By now the Qallunaat and their umiak had reached the floe edge. The two Qallunaat sat in the front and the back. The one in front would throw the harpoon and the killing spear. The one in the back would steer the boat.

They gestured to the four hunters to man the oars.

But Ooleepeeka's father refused.

"I don't know if they can hunt," he told the others. "I'm not getting in the boat unless I steer." He looked at Father. "And not unless you are throwing the harpoon."

"You're right," Father said. "We can't take chances. We have young people with us."

When it became clear the boat would not go anywhere until the hunters got their way, the strangers gave up their spots. The one in the front burst out in his Qallunaat language. He sounded angry. His voice sounded like a dog barking. The one in the back spoke quietly. He offered the first set of oars to the angry Qallunaaq. Then he took second position for himself, still speaking into the other one's ear. Maakut's son took the third pair of oars. Tuk had the rear oars, just in front of Ooleepeeka's father at the steering oar.

Just then, the first Qallunaaq pointed in the direction of the great boat. He was talking again, but he wasn't angry anymore. He seemed excited.

Everyone turned. From the tallest horn that rose out of the top of the boat, Tuk spotted a small white flag waving against the blue sky. The second Qallunaaq signaled that they should head out of the bay. The flag meant that a whale had been spotted in the strait.

Tuk was used to paddling around with other children in skin-covered umiat, but this was more serious. He didn't want to make a fool of himself and embarrass Father. The Qallunaat were tall. Tuk tried to make his strokes longer, to match theirs. He leaned farther forward and pulled farther back. By the time they reached the mouth of the bay, they were moving fast.

....

One of the oarsmen shouted. Everyone looked up.

Sure enough, Arvik's blowing could be seen in the distance — a stream of mist rising out of the water.

Ooleepeeka's father steered them through clumps of small ice cakes. He kept a wide distance from the big ones. It would not do to become trapped between two large moving ice floes.

Even though it was awkward, Tuk couldn't help turning to see what Father was doing at the front end of the boat. Father found the killing spear. It was attached by hooks to the inside ledge. He would need it later on. He examined the harpoon the Qallunaaq had given him. Tuk noticed that this harpoon's head seemed to be fixed to the shaft.

That was odd. It should be tied to the shaft with a loose knot. That way the shaft could be snapped away, leaving the head good and buried in the whale. Otherwise, the weight of the shaft might rip the harpoon head back out.

Several times, Father heaved the strangers' harpoon as if to throw it, then pulled it back. He was testing the weight and the feel of it. Father would know how to strike with it by the time they reached the whale.

The line attached to the harpoon was different from Father's line. It was thick and made up of many smaller lines all twisted together. Tuk hoped it was as strong as a seal-hide line.

The Qallunaat had no floats, either, Tuk noticed. They were going to rely on the extraordinary length of the line to tie the whale to them, like a dog to a sled. The line lay in a perfect coil at the bottom of the boat.

The second oarsman cautioned Tuk and Maakut's son to stay away from that coil. But Tuk didn't need to be told. He knew that if he got caught in it, he would be pulled out of the boat and dragged down with the whale, underwater forever.

After a short while, Father leaned out over the bow. He put a hand back and signaled for quiet. Arvik was under the water, but not very far.

All oars were raised from the water. Arvik had good hearing. He must not be alarmed.

Ooleepeeka's father checked the waves and fluttered the steering oar back and forth, back and forth. He made the boat move like a fish. The sea and wind currents carried them a little way. But soon the oars had to be gently dipped in and out, to nudge the boat into the right spot.

Father held himself still. He leaned out over the water, harpoon poised. Ooleepeeka's father guided the boat into position. Tuk knew that a good hunter feels, rather than sees, which way the whale will come up.

The Qallunaat watched the hunters work. From their positions at the oars, they had to twist their heads back and forth, between Ooleepeeka's father at the stern and Father over the bow. They squinted their eyes, and both their faces looked very stern.

Maybe they were worried, Tuk realized.

After all, we didn't trust them. Maybe they feel the same way about us.

Then several things happened all at once. Father sprang even farther out of the boat and struck the harpoon down, using both arms and all his strength. Tuk was afraid Father was going to lose his balance and fall out of the boat. But Father grabbed the edge with one hand and heaved himself back in.

At the helm, Ooleepeeka's father pushed hard on the steering oar. It groaned and wailed as it crunched against some pack ice floating under the surface.

Everyone winced. It was unthinkable that they might lose their steering oar.

In front, Maakut's son and the Qallunaat were pulling hard on one side, sending the boat into a backward turn. Tuk did the same.

SWOOSH! A wave of icy water caught them on the side and swamped the boat.

"Bail out, Tuk!" Ooleepeeka's father commanded. Tuk pulled in his oars and reached for the bucket that was tied behind his seat.

And as he turned, he saw the tail.

It rose out of the water. It blocked the sun. Like a black cliff, it towered over their tiny boat — the monster's tail.

Tuk froze. They were going to be smacked like mosquitoes.

"Bail now, Tuk!"

Tuk heard his father's voice from somewhere very far off. But he was surrounded by mist and ice.

Didn't Father see that he couldn't move? Didn't Father see the whale?

This was Arvik's world. They were too small. They were going to die.

But then a miracle happened. The great tail stopped its downward course in mid-air. It straightened and — *WHOOMP!* — dropped into the churning waters.

Tuk was jolted into action by the icy water sloshing around his ankles. He bailed seawater over the side. He saw Father step lightly around the line, which was now twisting and jumping. The line ripped itself from its coil as if it were alive. The weight of the whale pulled it out of the boat and down. The little

boat tossed in the thrashing water. Tuk bailed as fast as he could, but water kept sloshing back in.

Then one of the Qallunaat cried out, and Tuk looked over. A wisp of smoke was rising from the front of the boat.

The boat was on fire! How could it be?

"Pass the bucket up here!" Father called out, as he stepped back around the live line to get to the flames.

The line was being pulled too fast. The rope rubbing against the edge of the wooden boat was starting a fire!

Father quickly soaked the area. He kept pouring water on the rope after that.

"It looks like Arvik is in a mood to fight!" Ooleepeeka's father shouted over the waves. Even the Qallunaat seemed to understand what he meant.

Within moments, the rope reached its full length. It pulled at the metal ring that attached it to the bottom of the boat. With a lurch, the boat was dragged along. They tore through the loose ice on the end of a whale.

It was faster than anything Tuk could have imagined. He held on to his seat. This was a bumpy ride.

The wind whipped cold water and bits of ice at his face as they flew past. Everyone cringed at the sound — *SMACK!* — when the boat's hull hit solid ice.

But there was nothing they could do. Tuk opened his mouth and crunched down on the salty water in the air.

Maakut's son saw this and laughed.

"How do you like your first whale?" he shouted through the spray.

After a long time, their speed began to slow. Tuk relaxed his grip and flexed his cramped muscles. Ooleepeeka's father began to steer again. At this speed, it was possible to avoid the bigger chunks of pack ice.

"Arvik avoids open water," Father observed.

"He's clever, this fighter," agreed Ooleepeeka's father.

Tuk understood what they meant. Arvik must be trying to shake them loose amidst the ice. It was like bumping into rocks. Except the ice moved around. And you could never be sure where it would move next.

They were long out of sight of the great boat and the bay. It was a good thing there was no fog. The sun would show them the way back.

The boat came to a complete stop.

Had they lost Arvik? No, the line was still stretched tight. Father had driven the harpoon deep. Arvik must be resting down there, somewhere.

The second Qallunaaq reached into his coat and pulled out some black mud. To Tuk's surprise, he cut off a piece and put it in his mouth! The Qallunaaq chewed for a while and then spat a stream of black ooze into the water. He laughed at the expression on Tuk's face and offered him a piece.

Tuk shook his head. That was disgusting!

"I'll try." Maakut's son held out his hand. The Qallunaaq showed him how to chew and spit. Maakut's son popped the mud into his mouth, chewed and swallowed.

Right back up the whole mess came. Maakut's son vomited over the side of the boat. Ooleepeeka's father laughed and laughed. So did everyone else, a little bit. The only person who didn't think it was funny was Maakut's son.

"Awful stuff," he muttered. "Won't stay in the belly."

Suddenly, there was a *CRACK* and the low groan of wood under pressure. In no time, two large floes had shifted and wedged the boat between them. One floe was still pushing forward. The other wasn't budging.

Quickly, oars were pulled free of their oarlocks. Two men pushed on one side against the moving floe. Tuk and Maakut's son tried to push off the floe that was still. Father leaned out and did the same with the killing spear. The mud-eating Qallunaaq passed an oar to Ooleepeeka's father and grabbed a small ax that was fastened near his seat. He tried hacking chunks off the floe to remove some of the pressure on the boat.

The ax was sharp. It cut fast. Soon the

Qallunaaq jumped out of the boat on to the floe, so he could chop away even faster. For the moment, the boat floated free in a closed harbor of ice.

The Qallunaaq walked some distance to the far edge of the ice cake. It took a while. It was a big floe. He was looking for a good spot to try to hack a channel through the ice. There was nothing else to be done. If they were lucky, the ice would shift again and open up a pathway by itself.

Then something terrible happened.

It all happened so fast, yet each moment seemed to go on forever.

First, the line moved. It pulled straight down. Either Arvik was swimming deeper still, or the line was hooked under a huge piece of underwater ice. Whatever the reason, the boat was being pulled against its harbor of ice.

The boat started to tip to one side. The line was pulling hard. But this time, the boat had nowhere to go but down.

The Qallunaaq came running back to the

boat. He was waving the ax in the air. Tuk wished they could all just jump out of the boat on to the ice right there and then.

But he knew they couldn't lose the boat. They were too far out to sea. They would be stranded on the loose ice, waiting to be knocked into the water or to die of cold and wet — whichever came first.

Everyone scrambled to the high side of the boat. It kept tipping down anyway.

They had to cut the line, or Arvik would pull the boat underwater.

"Throw it, toss the ax to us!" Father yelled to the Qallunaaq, who was still a little way off. The man understood. He threw the tool at the boat. Everyone reached for it. They leaned far out of the high side of the boat.

It was a good throw. The ax flew in a high arc through the air and came down just shy of the high edge of the boat.

But there were too many hands reaching. Tuk lost sight of it for a moment, and then *THUNK*, and *SPLOSH!*

The ax slipped into the pool of sea below.

What terrible luck! Tuk didn't want to believe it. But he had no choice. The low side of the boat was being bent against the floe. It was making terrible snapping sounds. Soon it would take on water.

"My knife!" he yelled, pulling it from his pocket. "Father, my knife!"

Father grabbed Tuk's knife and eased his way down the boat, which was now pointing almost straight up in the air. Everyone else leaned farther out the high side to make up for the shift in weight. Father grabbed the end of the line and began to scrape Tuk's knife against it.

Scrape, scrape. Several strands of the line shredded apart. *Scrape, scrape.* More strands were cut through.

The boat groaned and wailed. The thick twist began to unravel.

SNAP!

SNAP!

SNAP!

The last few threads pulled apart. The high edge of the boat fell back into the water with a great *SPLASH* while everyone threw themselves toward the middle. They didn't want their weight to tip the boat over in the other direction.

They rested like that for a moment, in a heap. Then the Qallunaaq on the ice carefully climbed back into the boat.

5

WHEN the floes finally parted and they were on the way home, everyone was full of laughter. They laughed about Maakut's son eating the mud. Ooleepeeka's father imitated the look on Tuk's face when they were speeding through the pack ice. Everybody laughed.

They even laughed about the ax, and how it had disappeared into the water. And that wasn't even funny, not a bit.

What's more, they had lost a harpoon and

a great deal of perfectly good line. And they had failed to bring in the whale.

But at that moment, nobody minded any of it.

What an adventure! And every man who went out was coming back alive.

It was almost dark by the time they returned. It was the end of another long day.

Tuk found Grandfather outside the iglu. He was working on the kamotiq, pouring water from Mother's new kettle over the sled runners.

Tuk watched as Grandfather used a scrap of polar bear fur to smooth the hot water along them. The cold air quickly froze the water into a glossy layer of ice.

"I'm going inland tomorrow to look for spring caribou, if you want to come," Grandfather said.

Tuk shifted from one foot to the other. Normally he would have jumped at the chance to go on a hunting trip, just him and Grandfather. And tasting the first caribou of

the year was always a special treat, after a winter of seal meat.

But now there was the whale hunt. Father might let him go out again. Tuk might even be allowed to visit the Qallunaat's great boat! He wouldn't want to miss any of that.

"All right, you stay here," Grandfather said after a while. "You catch Arvik and I will pay my respects to the caribou."

Tuk couldn't tell if he was angry or not.

"Remember that we need caribou, too. We need caribou to come again at the end of the warm season, or we will have no clothes next winter."

"Yes, Grandfather. I will remember and I promise I will help with the fall hunt."

Then Grandfather smiled, but it was a sad sort of smile.

"I just hope we are all as sensible as you are, when the time comes."

Tuk hated it when Grandfather was sad. He searched for something to tell him, to distract him.

"Just yesterday I was scared of those

Qallunaat," he said. "And then today, out on the water… they became like friends. Samik's father was right about the hunt, but he was wrong, too. About the Qallunaat, I mean."

"You can learn a great deal from those men, both good and bad," Grandfather replied.

"But, Grandfather, I don't think they are bad at all."

Grandfather sighed and put down the kettle. He looked at Tuk. Then he looked at the kettle.

"I don't mean *they* are bad. They bring many things, is what I meant."

"Yes," said Tuk, touching his knife. "They bring good things."

"Many doesn't mean good and it doesn't mean bad," said Grandfather. "But many is rather a lot. We have our knowledge and our stories, but we don't have many things. One day that may change."

Tuk disagreed with Grandfather. They had the animals. Ptarmigan gave them feathers, flesh and their eggs. Seal and caribou gave them meat, fat, bones and skins. A polar bear skin kept them warm at night. The dogs pulled their sleds.

They had so many things. They had everything.

And now, Tuk had a knife.

Author's Note

....

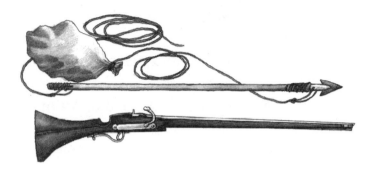

....

I BEGAN to imagine Tuk's story after reading the book *When the Whalers Were Up North: Inuit Memories from the Eastern Arctic*, by Dorothy Eber Harley. I was struck especially by an anecdote about a group of Inuit who were meeting American whalers for the first time. Their shaman had taken the precaution of casting a spell on the strangers, rendering them harmless so that the group felt it was safe to interact with them.

....

I wanted to invent a situation where both whalers and Inuit felt themselves to be on new and uncertain ground. So I set *Tuk and the Whale* in a much earlier time in Arctic whaling history — the beginning decades of the 1600s.

I imagined that Tuk and his family hunted over a large area on the eastern coast of what is now called Baffin Island. At this time, only a few Europeans would have been along this coast. Norse sailors would have come centuries before. Over the years the odd whaling ship had probably passed through. And by the end of the 1500s, England had started sending out explorers to search for mineral riches and a northern passage to Asia.

But to the south, across the Labrador Sea, European ships had been bringing whaling crews to Labrador and Newfoundland for some time. It was a very profitable, if risky, industry that harvested whale oil and baleen. Whale oil was used in various manu-facturing processes (leather, wool and the production of soap). It was also used to light the streets and buildings of European cities (in this sense, Ooleepeeka's father guesses correctly when he says the strangers have many qulliit). The whales' baleen was a strong and flexible material used for everything from carriage springs to corsets.

This story imagines what might have happened if the people of Tuk's camp encountered such European whalers, far from their usual whaling route, blown and buffeted by storms. The Europeans would likely be frightened as well as sick from a lack of fresh food. Perhaps they had lost men and valuable equipment. Even with these setbacks the whalers would be determined to bring back as many barrels of oil and as much "whalebone," or baleen, as possible. This was their livelihood.

Both the Inuit and the Europeans prized the bowhead whale, for different reasons. Each group could offer valuable contributions to the task of hunting them. Despite their differences, they might decide to hunt together — some two hundred years before such teamwork would become common-place in the Arctic.

There is much about Arctic life in the 1600s that is unknown to us today. When possible, *Tuk and the Whale* is informed by books and online sources. The reading list that follows outlines some of these. I'm lucky that Dr. David Morrison, Director of Archaeology and History at the Canadian Museum of Civilization, offered insight and advice when I couldn't find answers in the literature. I also feel very privileged that Dr. Robert McGhee, Curator of Arctic Archaeology at the Canadian Museum of Civilization, agreed to review the text and illustrations for errors. My thanks go to both of these experts.

Raquel Rivera

Glossary*

Arvik Bowhead whale, named for its bow-shaped jaw. A very large dark-colored whale, the bowhead was prized by early European whalers (and, later, by American whalers). They harvested only the blubber and baleen—the animal's mouth fringe that traps plankton.

Beluga Small white beaked whale, with a large rounded bump on its head.

Bola (throwing bones) What Tuk refers to as "throwing bones" are commonly known as bola. An Inuit bola is a weapon made of two, three or four weights (bone or ivory) tied to sinew cords. The weights are swung in the air and thrown at prey to trap it in the strings. It is used mostly for hunting birds.

Bow-drill Tool used for boring holes in wood, bone, stone, antler or ivory. A bowstring is looped

*There are a number of languages and dialects spoken across the North. Even in the same area, spelling in the Roman alphabet varies — different attempts to capture the sounds of the language. In this book, the Inuktitut words are only one of many possible versions.

....

around the drill shaft, making it spin fast as the bow is moved back and forth.

Floe edge A land floe (also known as the main floe) is sea ice that is attached to the shoreline. The open-water side of this ice mass is called the floe edge.

Ice floe Slab of ice floating on a body of water.

Iglu House, including a temporary house made of snow. Has been adopted into English usage to mean Inuit snowhouse.

Kamik, kamiit (pl.) Inuit boot (like iglu and kayak, kamik has been adopted into English usage, in which case the plural is kamiks).

Kamotiq Long sled made with slats of wood tied on to two runners. If wood was not available, animal skins could hold the load.

Kayak One-person boat, originally made with animal skin stretched over a driftwood frame.

Maktaaq The skin of whales.

Narwhal Small black-and-white speckled whale. Male narwhals grow a tusk (really a tooth) that looks like a unicorn horn.

Ptarmigan Arctic bird that turns white during winter. Ptarmigan have feathers on their feet, which help them to walk in snow.

Qallunaaq, Qallunaat (pl.) Thought perhaps to mean originally "one eyebrow" or "bushy eyebrows" in reference to the hairy faces of Europeans they encountered. It has come to mean all foreigners or non-Inuit.

Qulliq, qulliit (pl.) Stone lamp for burning animal fat. Used for heat, cooking and light.

Umiak, umiat (pl.) Boat made with skin stretched over a frame. Larger than a kayak, an umiak holds more people and goods for long-distance travel.

Yearling float Bag made from the skin of a yearling seal and filled with air.

Selected Sources

Saving the Endangered Caribou.
http://www.cbc.ca/news/background/caribou/

Boas, Franz. *The Central Eskimo*. Lincoln: University of Nebraska Press, 1964.

Eber, Dorothy Harley. *When the Whalers Were Up North: Inuit Memories from the Eastern Arctic*. Kingston, Montreal: McGill-Queen's University Press, 1989.

Ekho, Naqi and Ottokie, Uqsuralik. *Childrearing Practices*. Iqaluit: Nunavut Arctic College, 2000.

Fossett, Renée. *In Order to Live Untroubled: Inuit of the Central Arctic, 1550-1940.* Winnipeg: University of Manitoba Press, 2001.

Francis, Daniel. *Arctic Chase: A History of Whaling in Canada's North*. St. John's: Breakwater Books, 1984.

Harrington, Richard. *The Inuit: Life as It Was*. Edmonton: Hurtig Publishers, 1981.

Houston, James. *Confessions of an Igloo Dweller: Memories of the Old Arctic*. Toronto: McClelland & Stewart, 1995.

Jackson, C. Ian, ed. *The Arctic Whaling Journals of William Scoresby the Younger, Volume I, The Voyages of 1811, 1812, and 1813*. London: The Hakluyt Society, 2003.

Jenkins, J.T. *A History of the Whale Fisheries*. Port Washington, London: Kennikat Press, 1921.

McGhee, Robert. *The Arctic Voyages of Martin Frobisher: An Elizabethan Adventure*. Montreal, Kingston: Canadian Museum of Civilization/McGill-Queen's University Press, 2001.

Proulx, Jean-Pierre. *Whaling in the North Atlantic: From Earliest Times to the Mid-Nineteenth Century*. Ottawa: Parks Canada, 1986.

Ross, W. Gillies. *Arctic Whalers, Icy Seas: Narratives of the Davis Strait Whale Fishery*. Toronto: Irwin Publishing, 1985.

Verrill, A. Hyatt. *The Real Story of the Whaler: Whaling, Past and Present*. New York, London: D. Appleton and Company, 1923.

....

For Further Reading

Aboriginal Canada Portal: Kids
www.aboriginalcanada.gc.ca/acp/site.nsf/en/ao0
4607.html

Carrick, Carol. *Whaling Days*. New York: Clarion
Books, 1993.

Great Arctic Hunter Game
www.sila.nu/pub/swf/tgah/en/index.html

Hoyt-Goldsmith, Diane. *Arctic Hunter*. New York:
Holiday House, 1992.

Johnson, Christina. *Blue Whales and Other Baleen
Whales* (Animals of the World). Chicago: World
Book Inc., 2005.

Stanley, Diane. *The True Adventure of Daniel Hall*.
New York: Dial Books for Young Readers, 1995.